...r heart fluttered. How could she a state of Nature are equal, free and fluttered. ...he secure ...re are equal, free ...ndent...". ...could she ...freedom? ...e and indep... Free. Her cure her fre... ...nd in a state ...t...". Free. ...fluttered. "Mankind in a s... ...e equal, free ...rt fluttered. How could she secure ...re are equal, free and independent...". ...ld she secure her freedom? "Mankind

To Aura —G.W.

This book is for Phillip, Kristin, Georgette,
Jonah, Soraya, and Jonathan for all their
love and support. Thank You! —A.D.

Acknowledgments: On a bitterly cold January day, Barbara Dowling, historian
with the Trustees of Reservations, took me through the (unheated) Ashley
House in Sheffield, Massachusetts; warmly recounting dozens of anecdotes and
explanations about the Ashleys, Mumbet, and life in Sheffield; followed by a
driving tour to the places Mumbet lived and worked; and ending with a walk
to her final resting place in the Stockbridge cemetery. My good friend Ken
Barratt cheerfully shivered along with me and took loads of pictures. Barbara
and fellow historian Will Garrison read early drafts of the manuscript and
answered many questions. David Levinson, coauthor with Emilie Piper of the
definitive biography of Mumbet, filled in more details during final revisions.
Andrew Karre has been a most congenial editor, and Alix Delinois's illustrations
are a joy to behold. Many thanks to them all. —G.W.

Carolrhoda Books
A division of Lerner Publishing Group, Inc.
241 First Avenue North
Minneapolis, MN 55401 U.S.A.

Website address: www.lernerbooks.com

The portrait of Elizabeth 'Mumbet' Freeman is used with the permission of:
© Massachusetts Historical Society, Boston, MA/The Bridgeman Art Library.

Main body text set in HandySans 18/24.

Library of Congress Cataloging-in-Publication Data

Woelfle, Gretchen, author.
    Mumbet's Declaration of Independence / by Gretchen Woelfle ; Illustrated by Alix Delinois.
        p.   cm.
    Summary: Mumbet's Declaration of Independence tells the story of a Massachusetts
slave from the Revolutionary era—in 1781, she successfully used the new Massachusetts
Constitution to make a legal case that she should be free.
    ISBN 978-0-7613-6589-1 (lib. bdg. : alk. paper)
    ISBN 978-1-4677-2399-2 (eBook)
    1. Freeman, Elizabeth, 1744?-1829—Juvenile literature. 2. Women slaves—Massachusetts—
Biography—Juvenile literature. 3. Slaves—Massachusetts—Biography—Juvenile literature.
4. African American women—Massachusetts—Biography—Juvenile literature.
5. Massachusetts—Biography—Juvenile literature. 6. Slavery—Massachusetts—History—
18th century—Juvenile literature. I. Delinois, Alix, illustrator. II. Title.
E444.F87W64 2014
306.3'62092—dc23 [B]   2013018620

Manufactured in the United States of America
1 - DP - 12/31/13

MUMBET'S
DECLARATION
OF INDEPENDENCE

BY
GRETCHEN
WOELFLE

ILLUSTRATIONS BY
ALIX DELINOIS

 CAROLRHODA BOOKS • MINNEAPOLIS

Mumbet didn't have a last name
because **she was a slave.**

She didn't even have an official first name. Folks called her Bett or Betty. Children fondly called her Mom Bett or Mumbet. Others weren't so kind.

Colonel John **Ashley** was the richest man in Berkshire **C**ounty, Massachusetts. He owned an iron mine, a forge, a sawmill, a gristmill, a general store, and three thousand acres of farm and woodland.

He also **owned** Mumbet.

The colonel's wife, Mrs. **Ashley**, owned the sharpest tongue in town. **All** day she hurled spiteful names at Mumbet. She called her:

"Useless baggage..."
"Stubborn wench..."
"Dumb creature..."

"Don't mind her jabs, Lizzy," Mumbet said
to her daughter. "Look at that mountain
out there. Rain and wind, ice and snow try
to wear it down, but there it stands, strong
and rugged. Just like us." She stroked
Lizzy's curls and grinned.

What Mumbet did mind was someone owning her. Everyone in town worked hard, and many people worked on their own farms. Even servants and hired hands could choose to leave a cruel master. But Mumbet didn't have a choice. She was a "servant for life."

She gazed at the river running free
at the bottom of the meadow.
Freedom!
She thought of it day and night.

One day Mumbet kneaded bread dough, with Lizzy by her side. Glowing coals heated the oven. When it was hot enough, Mumbet shoveled out the coals and put in the bread to bake. Lizzy formed her own little loaf from leftover scraps of dough.

Mrs. Ashley came in and screamed
at Lizzy.
   "Thief! How dare you steal my food!"
She raised the coal shovel to strike the
girl, but Mumbet stuck out her arm
to take the blow.
   Crack! Blood spurted from her arm.
   Lizzy shrieked.
   Mrs. Ashley stared.

Mumbet wrapped a rag round the wound until the bleeding stopped. All winter long, the cut festered, but she never covered it. The wound was her badge of bravery.

Folks asked, "Why, Mumbet, what ails your arm?"

"Ask Madam," she replied.

Mrs. Ashley scowled. Mumbet's wound was her badge of shame.

In spring Mumbet watched the river break free of ice and flood the meadow. If only she could break free. If she could have one minute in her life, just to say "I am free..."

"Scrub that kettle," snapped Mrs. Ashley. Mumbet scrubbed and chuckled. Mrs. Ashley didn't own the river of thoughts that ran through Mumbet's head.

Others were thinking about freedom too. Americans didn't like the laws and taxes Britain forced on them. Town leaders met in Colonel Ashley's study.

"Take the men some food and drink," ordered Mrs. Ashley.

Voices rang out as Mumbet entered the room.

"The King means to take away our rights!" one man shouted.

Do I have rights? wondered Mumbet.

"He would make us slaves!" cried another man.

You wouldn't like that. Not one bit, thought Mumbet.

Colonel Ashley turned to a young lawyer with fire in his eyes. "Write this down, Mr. Sedgwick: 'Mankind in a state of Nature are equal, **free, and independent** . . .'"

Mumbet set down her tray.

Wasn't she a part of mankind?

"...the great end of society is to secure those rights wherewith God and Nature have made us free."

Free. Her heart fluttered.

How could she secure her freedom?

The town held a parade when the American colonies declared their independence from Britain. Then local men marched off to war for seven long years, to keep hold of that independence.

Thwack! Thwack! Mumbet pounded flax stalks until the fiber came free.
   If she could have one minute of freedom, she would be willing to die at
the end of that minute.
   Thwack! Just to stand one minute on the earth as a free woman!
   Thwack! Mumbet would be free, but how?

The town held a meeting to learn about the Massachusetts Constitution—the new law of the land. Mumbet slipped into the back of the hall. She couldn't see over the crowd, but she heard well enough.

"All men are born free and equal."

Mumbet wrinkled her brow. Was this law meant for her?

The next day she picked up a shopping basket, but she walked past the store. Mumbet stopped at the crossroads. Perhaps her plan would fail, and Mrs. Ashley would treat her worse than ever. She would take that chance. She would go to the young lawyer with fire in his eyes, Mr. Theodore Sedgwick.

"Mumbet, what are you doing here?" he asked.

Right then she made her declaration of independence. "I want to be free. I've got a *right* to be free."

Mr. Sedgwick's eyebrows shot up. "What gives you such a notion?"
"The new constitution says so: all people are born free and equal," Mumbet replied. "I am not a dumb creature. I deserve my freedom."

Mr. Sedgwick rubbed his chin. "I don't know…"

"You wrote those freedom words at Colonel Ashley's house," she said. "Do you believe them?" Her blazing eyes met his.

"Of course, but that was not the law…"

"The new constitution is the law." Mumbet folded her arms.

"Yes, but…" He gazed at Mumbet standing strong as a mountain and pounded his desk. "We will go to court together and test the new law. But if we lose…"

"I will be no worse off," Mumbet said, "and if we win, I will be free!"

A few days later, a loud knock sent Mumbet to the front door.

"Colonel John Ashley," said the sheriff, holding out a paper.

Colonel Ashley read it and exclaimed, "Give up Mumbet? She's my property. You know that."

"You refuse?" asked the sheriff.

"Of course I do."

"Good day then, Colonel," said the sheriff.

Mrs. Ashley slammed the door.

Mumbet hid a smile. Her fight for freedom had begun!

Mumbet and Mr. Sedgwick entered the courthouse on a hot August day. The room was crowded with their neighbors.

Colonel Ashley argued that he had owned Mumbet for many years. She was his servant for life.

Mr. Sedgwick argued that even though people owned slaves in Massachusetts, no law had ever made it legal. Now the new constitution made it illegal. Mumbet was not anyone's "servant for life."

The jury and judge thought it over and agreed.

Mumbet was free, and so was Lizzy!

"I suppose I'll have to pay you wages now," snapped Mrs. Ashley. "No, you won't," said Mumbet. "I'm quitting your house forever!"

Mumbet returned to the courthouse one more time—to choose two names for herself. From that day on, she was Elizabeth Freeman, and for the rest of her long life, she lived free as a river and strong as a mountain.

AUTHOR'S NOTE

Mumbet became the housekeeper, midwife, nurse, and second mother to Theodore Sedgwick's large family. When the Sedgwick children were grown, Mumbet lived out her days with her own daughter, grandchildren, and great-grandchildren. She was laid to rest in the Sedgwick burial plot in Stockbridge, Massachusetts, and her gravestone reads:

ELIZABETH FREEMAN
known by the name of
Mumbet
died December 28, 1829
Her supposed age
Was 85 Years

She was born a slave and remained a slave for nearly thirty years. She could neither read nor write yet in her own sphere she had no superior or equal. She neither wasted time nor property. She never violated a trust nor failed to perform a duty. In every situation of domestic trial, she was the most efficient helper, and the tenderest friend. Good mother, farewell.

Mumbet's Story

Mumbet left no record of her life. We have Catharine Maria Sedgwick, her lawyer's daughter, to thank for writing Mumbet's story. Catharine described Mumbet in letters, journals, and an essay called "Slavery in New England."

Other Massachusetts slaves had gained their freedom in court from masters who had broken promises to free them. Colonel Ashley gave Mumbet no such promise. Her 1781 court case challenged the legality of slavery itself. Two years later, a judge declared slavery unconstitutional in Massachusetts, and soon after that, all five thousand slaves in the state gained their freedom.

Mumbet's Mysteries

There is much we don't know about Mumbet. When was she born? Where? Who were her parents? We know that Mumbet had been owned by Mrs. Ashley's father in New York State, but we don't know when she came to Massachusetts. Some stories say that Lizzy was Mumbet's sister, but more likely, she was her daughter. One legend says Mumbet had a husband who died fighting in the American Revolution.

Perhaps the most intriguing story comes from W. E. B. DuBois, a champion for African American civil rights a hundred years ago and the first African American to earn a PhD from Harvard. He claimed that Mumbet married his great-grandfather late in life.

Historians have found no records of Mumbet's exact age, her parents, her marriage to a soldier, or a marriage to DuBois's ancestor. Yet what we do know about Mumbet is more important than what we don't know. Catharine Sedgwick wrote, "Mumbet had a clear and nice perception of justice and a stern love of it, an uncompromising honesty in word and deed, and conduct of high intelligence."

Mumbet Today

History is fluid, like the Housatonic River flowing through Berkshire County. Ashley House still stands, now open to the public. Not long ago, tour guides focused on Ashley, his wealth, and service to town, colony, and state. He was the hero of Ashley House, and Mumbet was just a footnote. Today, when people visit Ashley House, they hear much more about Mumbet, the slave who stood up to the most powerful man in town. She is also part of the regional African American Heritage Trail and the star of a Mumbet Day Celebration held each August 21, the anniversary of her freedom trial.

Massachusetts Constitution of 1780

These are the words that prompted Mumbet to go to court to win her freedom:

Article I. All men are born free and equal, and have certain natural, essential, and unalienable rights; among which may be reckoned the right of enjoying and defending their lives and liberties; that of acquiring, possessing, and protecting property; in fine, that of seeking and obtaining their safety and happiness.

Susan Ridley Sedgwick, Catharine's sister-in-law, painted a small portrait of Mumbet (left, actual size) which is now in the Massachusetts Historical Society in Boston.

SELECTED BIBLIOGRAPHY

Dewey, Mary, ed. *The Power of Her Sympathy: The Autobiography and Journal of Catharine Maria Sedgwick.* Boston: Massachusetts Historical Society, 1993.

Piper, Emilie, and David Levinson. *One Minute a Free Woman: Elizabeth Freeman and the Struggle for Freedom.* Great Barrington, MA: Upper Housatonic Valley National Heritage Area / African American Heritage Trail, 2010.

Wilds, Mary. *Mumbet: The Life and Times of Elizabeth Freeman.* Greensboro, NC: Avisson Press, 1999.

Zilversmit, Arthur. "Mumbet: Folklore and Fact." *Berkshire History* 1, no. 1 (Spring 1971): 2-14.

——. "Quok Walker, Mumbet, and the Abolition of Slavery in Massachusetts." *William and Mary Quarterly*, 3rd ser., 25, no. 4 (October 1968): 614-624.

FURTHER READING

BOOKS

Nelson, Vaunda Micheaux. *Bad News for Outlaws: The Remarkable Life of Bass Reeves, Deputy U.S. Marshal.* Minneapolis: Carolrhoda Books, 2009.

Rockwell, Anne. *Hey, Charleston! The True Story of the Jenkins Orphanage Band.* Minneapolis: Carolrhoda Books, 2013.

WEBSITES

www.mumbet.com
This site reproduces the court transcript of Mumbet's trial and her will, as well as photos of Mumbet sites. Some information on the site has not been confirmed by historians.

www.thetrustees.org/places-to-visit/berkshires/ashley-house.html
The staff at Ashley House continues to research Mumbet's life and holds an annual Mumbet Day Celebration on August 21.

www.uhvafamtrail.org
The Upper Housatonic Valley African American Heritage Trail takes in Ashley House and Stockbridge Cemetery, as well as sites related to other prominent African Americans.

www.masshist.org/endofslavery/index.cfm
The Massachusetts Historical Society website includes objects from Mumbet's life and an essay, "African Americans and the End of Slavery in Massachusetts."

free and independent . . ." Free. He... secure her freedom? "Mankind in independent . . ." Free. Her heart her freedom? "Mankind in a state of Natu... Free. Her heart fluttered. How... "Mankind in a state of Nature are equal, fre... heart fluttered. How could she se... of Nature are equal, free and independe... How could she secure her freedom? and independent . . ." Free. Her hea... her freedom? "Mankind in a state of Natu... Free. Her heart fluttered. How co...